The MAD SURVIVAL HANDBOOK

Written by
Stan Hart

Illustrated by
Paul Coker

Edited by
Nick Meglin

WARNER BOOKS

A Warner Communications Company

This book is dedicated to four people. The
first two are our son Christopher and our
daughter Victoria who have found ways of
surviving while living in the same house with
my wife Joan and me.

The third and fourth people are my wife Joan
and me who have found ways of surviving
while living in the same house with
Christopher and Victoria.

S.H.

WARNER BOOKS EDITION

Copyright © 1980 by Stan Hart, Paul Coker,
and E.C. Publications, Inc.

This Warner Books Edition is published by
arrangement with E.C. Publications, Inc.

Warner Books, Inc.,
75 Rockefeller Plaza,
New York, N.Y. 10019

 A Warner Communications Company

Printed in the United States of America

First Printing: September, 1980

10 9 8 7 6 5 4 3 2 1

CONTENTS

ENEMIES I

In order to survive, first you should know who the enemies to your survival are! Therefore, it's important that you memorize the following "Enemies List"...

Probably the greatest threat to your survival is in your own home—your **parents!**

Uncles, aunts and cousins can make your life miserable beyond belief, if you don't know how to handle them...

You still wet your bed, Stevie?

I used to diaper him!

Hey, your face is starting to clear up...

Skylab, where are you when I need you?

Instead of going to the next family meeting, it might be more comfortable if you came down with the **plague!**

A serious threat to your survival is something you have absolutely no **control** over! It's known as "The Sibling Syndrome" or in plain English, "Those lousy brothers and sisters of yours."

An enemy who threatens your slobbish way of life with extinction is the neat kid who lives next door! Your mother will never stop wondering, "Why can't you be like him?"

See how **nice** Rodger looks! Why can't **you** look this nice, Harold?

You should see how nice he looks when he wears his sister's dress!

9

10

Now that you've learned who some of
your **enemies** are, let's take a look at
some of the BATTLEGROUNDS on
which your fight for survival
will be fought...

BATTLEGROUNDS
I

BATTLEGROUND:
The Dinner Table

ANALYSIS: The four combatants obviously should *never* be assembled in one place at one time since tensions are created that must be vented in sarcasm (father), shouting (mother), self-righteousness (daughter) and general loathing (son)! The happy family is the family that eats dinner at the same time, miles away from each other!

BATTLEGROUND:
The Family Car

ANALYSIS: The family car is like the family dinner table with wheels! The same antagonisms and hatreds that make dining such a torment, make driving even *worse!* How could it *possibly* be worse? Simple! At the dinner table, your mother doesn't criticize the way your father *eats*—in the car she positively OD's on the way he *drives!* What can you do to survive these ordeals? Why not day-dream erotic fantasies? Chances are your father will, too, once the shouting dies down.

BATTLEGROUND:
The School Gym

ANALYSIS: Here is a location that spells *disaster* for you, unless you're one of those Jocks— but if you were, you wouldn't be worrying about survival and reading this book, in the first place! Shall we go on? Well, the school gym is a *double* danger to your survival! First, when you can't even get your butt off the ground on the rope climb, and then later, in the shower room when all the other boys see you trying to cover up that pitiful naked body of yours! Use any trick you can think of to stay out of gym class! Don't say you haven't been warned*!!*

BATTLEGROUND:
Church

ANALYSIS: Sleeping in church is like giving God a *hot foot!* It might seem funny to some, but supposing The Almighty doesn't have a great sense of humor? The phrase "burn baby, burn" takes on a whole *new meaning!* It's bad enough to fall asleep during a sermon, but who can guarantee that you won't *talk* in your sleep?

ACADEMY AWARDS

Here we are among the greats and the ingrates of Hollywood! Tonight we're presenting awards to the best **actors!** Not the clods you see on the screen, but the everyday folks who by their acting skills survive year in and year out! And now, on with the show...

23

24

25

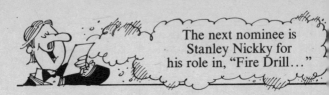

26

And the winner is, Alf Boni for his great work in, "My Father, The Godfather".

What kind of grades do you get in school?

Pretty good...

Ever been in trouble with the police?

Naw, with my old man, it couldn't happen!

Oh, is he a policeman or judge?

27

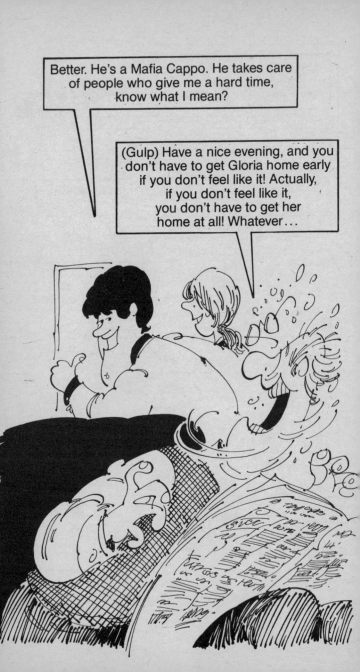

In the category, "The School", our first nominee is Larry Lynde for his pantomime performance in, "Just The Smell Of A Hot School Lunch Makes Me Faint…"

The next nominee is a shared nomination for both Alvin Brown and Rog Feversham for their wonderful roles in, "The Blackboard Eraser Cleaners…"

I sent you downstairs to clean the blackboard erasers, not to have an eraser fight!

Fight? **We** fight? We fought to keep your erasers from being stolen, right, Alvin?

Right!

31

And the winner, by a large margin, is Andrea Gustafsen for her magnificent portrayal of a troubled teenager in, "My Parents Would Die If They Knew…"

Andrea, there's no excuse! You have to get into your gym clothes.

But Miss Mc Cardle…

…No "Buts", Andrea, do as I say!

Can I tell you why I don't want to be in gym class? It's because of a **health problem!**

What health problem do you have?

33

In the category, "Summer Camp", the first nominee is "Uncle" Shelly Burnbaum for his inspired performance in "It's Not What It Looks Like…"

All right, boys and girls, who can tell me which **Karate** hold I'm using to subdue "Aunt" Sharon? Come on, we had a Karate lesson last week, did you **forget** so soon?

SURVIVAL QUIZ

This section will tell you if you're prepared to survive or not. You get ten points for every correct answer and ten points for every incorrect answer. In other words, **who cares?**

When you tear your toenail and it starts to rip down instead of across, you should:

a) Stop;
b) Try to get it to rip upwards;
c) Keep going and use the bloody toe as an excuse to get out of gym class.

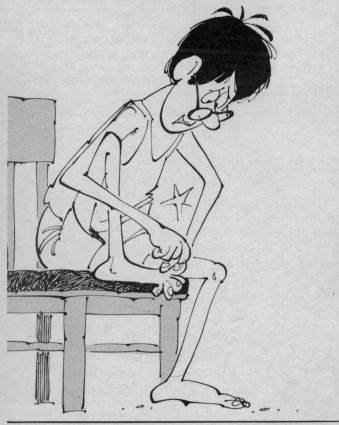

ANSWER: (c) Bet you knew this was the correct answer because it was the longest, right?

When you must have a piano lesson, you will get through it better if you:

a) Practice beforehand;
b) Have a nervous breakdown;
c) Blow in your piano teacher's ear and try to get her "excited".

ANSWER: (b) Actually (c) is much better, but you can't have two questions in a row with the same letter as an answer.

If you get a job as a peanut vendor in a ballpark, and on your first day, you're throwing peanuts all over the stands, you could:

a) Yell, "The treats on me!", and pay for the peanuts yourself; b) Call out, "I'm not much of an athlete, but I have a 3.8 grade point average."; c) Apply for welfare.

ANSWER: All of the above.

If you're peeping and you're caught by your father, immediately:

a) Say, "Wanna see something great, Pop?";
b) Tell dad that you're going to report the girl for wasting too much water; c) Pray that she doesn't see you when dear old dad turns on the light.

If you are ice skating and showing off your great form and suddenly remember you forgot to put on underpants, you should:

a) Pray that God strikes you dead before you hit the ground; b) Deny everything;
c) Pretend that you knew it all along.

ANSWER: *None of the above. There is no answer. Your entire life has just been ruined!*

When you're taking a bath and your little brother comes into the bathroom with a friend, you could:

a) Take a deep breath and submerge until they're gone; b) Get up and scare them off by showing your yicchy body; c) Scream and keep screaming until your parents send him away to a military academy.

ANSWER: *Any answer that works to get rid of the brat is acceptable!*

When you have to bathe your dog, you should:

a) Give him a dollar and let him go to a public bath ; b) Feign a cold and let your sister do it; c) Sell your interest in the dog to your brother the day before a bath is due.

ANSWER: a)....(Ed. Note: So it doesn't make any sense, so what?)

When you bring home the guy you're crazy about and he has table manners that make a sow look classy, you should:

a) Blame it on your parents because they made him nervous; b) Eat just like he's eating; c) Go into the kitchen, turn on the oven and put your head in it.

ANSWER: a) After all, what are parents for, if not for furnishing a good excuse for anything bad that happens?

When you've spent $15 trying to get the baseball card of your favorite player and your friend got him after spending only 25¢, you ought to:

a) Give up baseball and take up ballet; b) Give up your friend; c) Blame your parents.

You have taken your father's Playboy Magazine and are reading it, when the old man comes into your room. You should:

a) Confess that the pictures of naked girls mean nothing to you and that you need psychiatric help at $75 an hour; b) Tell him that you'd rather see pictures of naked men; c) Tell him that you need some pictures for your hygiene class project.

ANSWER: *None of the above. He's smart enough to know just how horny kids are.*

You're taking a test and you are caught looking at your neighbor's paper. You could:

a) Tell the teacher you're checking to see if your neighbor took his answers from you; b) Tell him you have a kink in your neck that you're trying to get rid of; c) Tell him that you're cheating.

ANSWER: c). Being honest is such an unexpected maneuver, that he will be too shocked to do anything.

SURVIVORS THROUGH HISTORY

Through history there have been some real great survivors! How about taking a look at them? What's your options? Well, if you don't want to, you could use this section as a scratch pad for notes on "Things You Have To Do This Week"...

RICHARD M. NIXON

The only man to have survived the Watergate scandal without ever going to jail or to trial...

HERBERT HOOVER

The President who went through the beginning of the depression saying "Prosperity is just around the corner," when actually what was "just around the corner" was a lot of people selling apples...

GEORGE WASHINGTON

The man who started the French and Indian War in America by accidentally firing on French diplomats and who survived this goof to become the first President of the United States! There's a message here, somewhere...

U.S. GRANT

Commemorating one of our nation's most famous drunks who came out of virtual retirement to command the Union forces to victory! How's that for surviving?

THE SHAH OF IRAN

The man who was deposed by his poverty-stricken countrymen and who must suffer living in exile in unimaginable splendor!

IDI AMIN

To the ugly slob who ruled Uganda with merciless cruelty, but got out without even a scratch when his people revolted. Who said, "Everyone loves a Fat Man"?

TALLEYRAND

One of the best survivors of all time was
this French diplomat. He lasted through
the French Revolution and was in power
no matter who came and went; Robes-
pierre, Marat, Napoleon. A true hero of
survival—dom.

BILL GAINES,
MAD MAGAZINE PUBLISHER

Talking about great survivors, how about
the man who sells trash to kids and gets
away with the scam, year after year!

ALBUM OF SURVIVAL GOOFS

Since I'm a snoop at heart, I've sneaked around, snapping pictures of the worst Survival Goofs I could find. Can you locate yourself in any of them?

You tried to impress a good-looking girl with what a swell guy you are and volunteered to walk her dog. Unfortunately, the dog ran away and never came back!

WHAT TO DO??? WHAT TO DO???

Follow the dog's example!

You hand in a report on a
book you didn't read and
think you're going to get
away with it. What makes
you think the teacher didn't
read the book, stupid?

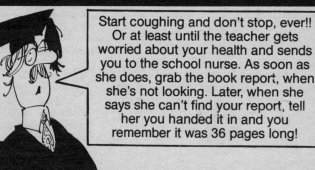

Start coughing and don't stop, ever!!
Or at least until the teacher gets
worried about your health and sends
you to the school nurse. As soon as
she does, grab the book report, when
she's not looking. Later, when she
says she can't find your report, tell
her you handed it in and you
remember it was 36 pages long!

You made a BRILLIANT dive from the high BoaRd and plunged deep into the pool. Unfortunately, your Bathing suit didn't follow you! It's floating right their on top...

You could do one of two things; One: Try deep breathing exercises while standing on the bottom of the pool; or Two: Get out of the pool, naked and say, "Gee, I thought folks around here were **modern!**". It doesn't make sense, but you can't afford to quibble, with your bareness waving in the breeze!

You're a school MONITOR and your
BEST friends have just BROKEN a
school RULE. The assistant
PRINCIPAL is watching. If you
REPORT them, you're a dead fink.
If you don't, you're a RETIRED
MONITOR!

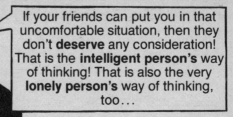

WHAT TO DO??? WHAT TO DO???

If your friends can put you in that
uncomfortable situation, then they
don't **deserve** any consideration!
That is the **intelligent person's** way
of thinking! That is also the very
lonely person's way of thinking,
too...

You Left your diary unlocked and
those two people who claim to be
your parents (how can you ever
know for sure, it's their word
against yours) are reading it...

You can tell them you're writing a
novel and that it's all **fiction**! Or, you
can make history by becoming the
first child to ever put herself up for
adoption!

You waited till the last minute to pick up your prom dress from the cleaners. In fact, you waited past the last minute...

You could go to the paint store instead. **Paint** store? **Paint store!** Get some red paint, put daubs of it all over your body and when your prom date calls, tell him you have **measles!** Then settle back and think of the least painful ways to kill yourself!

You're at a party and you go to the bathroom. Nothing wrong with that — some pretty important people go to the bathroom. But sometimes the sound of the toilet flushing is a source of intense merriment to the others at the party...

WHAT TO DO??? WHAT TO DO???

Why not pick out the clown who's leading the laughter and say, "Gosh, Freddie (whoever,) I hate having to flush after you every time you go to the bathroom. It's about time you did it yourself!"

You have a date with a nice, new fellow and you meet a girlfriend of yours. Somehow your mind goes BLANK and you forget the young man's name!

WHAT TO DO??? WHAT TO DO???

When you leave your friend, tell the guy that you didn't want your girlfriend to know his name. You're the **possesive** type and you know how he turns girls on! (Note: You might have to pay for this lie when you try to send him home, later that night!)

You and your Boyfriend have gone to a drive-in for some flicks and some making-out. Unfortunately in the next car are your Mother and father sneakily watching you watch the flicks and making sure you <u>don't</u> make out!

WHAT TO DO??? WHAT TO DO???

Get out of the car and go into the back seat of **their** car with your boyfriend. You see, parents never want you to **know** that they're snooping! So they will not turn around to see what you're doing in the back of their car. You're safe to do **anything** you want to!

You exchange Christmas gifts
with your Best friend and
she gives you the same present
that you Bought for her at a
"Half-Price Sale"!

Tell your friend that you bought her present **months ago** when you first saw it and kept it until now! She **might** believe you, but will you believe her when she tries to tell you the same rotten lie?

You have a low-cut gown
for the prom. You drop a
flower and try to pick it up.
Everyone stops and looks
as you bend over...

You could be tough and say, "What's
the matter, haven't you ever seen
jugs before?" On second thought...
you shouldn't feel threatened. Think
of the attention as a **compliment!**

You have a low-cut gown
for the prom. You drop a
flower and try to pick it up.
No one stops and looks
as you bend over...

WHAT TO DO??? WHAT TO DO???

You could call out, "Free show!!", but
you might be setting everyone up for
a big disappointment! Maybe the best
thing is to go to the coatroom and
put a sweater on over the gown and
wait a few years...

IT'S BETTER TO DIE THAN....

Shake hands with your uncle who
has just been picking his nose!

IT'S BETTER TO DIE THAN....

Live with your telephone number written in indelible ink on a telephone booth wall!

IT'S BETTER TO DIE THAN....

Have your stomach make noises when you're out with the best looking guy in school!

IT'S BETTER TO DIE THAN....

Not remember whether or not you used
deodorant before you went dancing!

IT'S BETTER TO DIE THAN....

Decorate your date's carpet with
what's stuck on your shoe!

ENEMIES II

Up to now, I've shown you enemies who threaten your existence just for the **fun** of it! Now, here are a group of villains who are stalking your well-being for **money!** Check out these **professional** enemies...

One of the many things the world **doesn't** need is **The Mens' Room Attendant!** If you're old enough to go to the bathroom by yourself, you're probably old enough to wash your hands without anyone's help! So, if you allow yourself to become intimidated (a very big threat to survival) by an old guy with a tiny hand towel, you're near the brink of self-destructing!

It takes one to know one, so I can speak with authority! The reason why anyone would want a lousy paying job like being a **teacher** is so they can have a sense of power and make your life miserable! Whenever you can, avoid teachers...

Well did you or did you not read the assignment for today?

Could I go outside for a minute and throw myself in front of traffic?

That's the coward's way, shame on you!

88

Just a word of encouragement to you ordinary looking girls out there! Just because the zowie looking **model** in the breathtakingly tight sweater gathers guys like a flame gathers moths, don't think your life is at an end! There are **many things** you can do to attract the boys away from that luscious vision… although at the moment, I can't think of a single one…

The feeling of **guilt** is a real survival killer! So beware! There are those among us who will stir up your latent guilt feelings for their own gain...*

If you only want to give me a quarter, that's all right! Who cares if I die because I couldn't afford a place to sleep tonight?

How about a dollar?

Well, if it'll make you feel any better, okay...

* Like book publishers who ask, "Why are you reading this at the book rack instead of buying it?"

On "The Survival Enemies" list, near the top
is The Waiter—a very grave threat to your
sanity! While you're blowing a bundle on dinner,
he makes you feel like he's doing you a favor
by **waiting** on you! Then he makes you feel like
a cretin if you ask for his assistance and then he
really makes you feel self-loathing when you overtip
him after all that abuse!

BATTLEGROUNDS II

Here are more **battlegrounds** and scenes of combat! Cough, cough, if I don't pull through, give my medals to my kid brother and tell that freckled face tyke...

Knock it off, creep!

BATTLEGROUND:
The Lawn

ANALYSIS: The lawn takes the battle for survival *outdoors!* It's been your job to mow the lawn and water it! You've done *neither*, because you're a kid, and anyone with a little bit of smarts knows that kids never do what they're supposed to do! So get ready for a couple of hours of operatic howling by your old lady and a couple of days of scowling by your tiresome old man! They're staging their *attacks* on your survival! Be brave... also be quiet! It'll all *blow over!* They can't legally throw you out of the house until you're eighteen!

BATTLEGROUND:
A Co-ed Party

ANALYSIS: *Immoral behavior* can be a great challenge to your survival! Not *your* immoral behavior, the immoral behavior of *that* girl in your class! All the boys want to put their hands on her! So they flock around her and ignore everyone else! But don't forget, you still have *your* spotless reputation to enjoy—even if you have to enjoy it all by *yourself!*

BATTLEGROUND:
The Crowded Bus

ANALYSIS: Can that part of you that feels you are a decent human being survive a bus trip with an old lady standing while you sit and try to ignore her? If not, then get up and give her your seat—and put down this book, you're *wasting* your time! But if you can survive this test, you're our kind of folks! Hell, she ought to ride during *off-hours* anyway, right? *Sure!* To avoid angry stares when you get up, you could look blankly ahead of you and grope your way off the bus and pretend you've got *worse* problems! *Dumping Guilt* is a wonderful strategy for offensive survival!

ANALYSIS: If you are unlucky enough to be in a school play, you will get a chance to experience what *death* is all about! The audience is out there just waiting for you to 1) Make a mistake; and/or 2) Come on stage with your fly open!

"Survival in Theater" is a whole branch of survival that can't be fully examined here! Just a hint or two: if you *fail*, your friends in the theater will feel bad; if you succeed, your friends will feel even *worse!*

BATTLEFIELD:
Porno Theater.

ANALYSIS: There's only one thing worse than being caught in the act—being caught when you haven't done anything at all! How are you going to make your Aunt believe you were just *passing by*? You can't, so you may as well use *another* attack! Something like, "Hi, Auntie Em, I was just sitting next to Uncle Harry *inside!*"

A DAY IN THE LIFE OF...

Oh, **there** you are! I'm so glad you could join me! Just keep a little quiet so she doesn't pull down the shades before finishing her shower! But seriously, what do you say we take a gander at a "Day in the Life of a Survivor—**Kid Division**..."

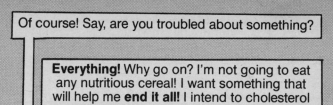

Naturally, our survivor is not prepared for school, but he will overcome...

I never knew your eyes were so **blue!**

Please, don't...

Blue as the Aegean at sunset! Ah, to be on the Aegean at sunset with you...

Stop this!

Because he's out so many nights, his parents have decided that he should stay home week nights and only go out on **weekends!** How does he counter that? Easy...

Oh, It's me, simply me! I adore staying home! I can try on all of mom's clothes and sis's underwear and stockings! I'm all goose bumps!

Okay, here's our **Adult Division!** Here our **adult**
not only believes in surviving, he also
believes in surviving **upwards!** But
between him and where he wants to go are
some other people in the company…

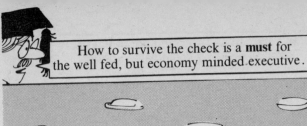

How to survive the check is a **must** for the well fed, but economy minded executive...

After spending a jolly afternoon with a secretary at a motel, our hero runs the risk of being **found out** by his wife! But if he did get found out, then he wouldn't be "Our Hero" would he? Watch how he survives **this** encounter...

What's that dear?

It came from your pocket! What were you doing in the Boom Boom Motel?

Oh that? I went there with my secretary!

You **admit** it?

Of course, I admit it! We went there so we could get some **work done** and not be interrupted by the phone all the time like we are in the office!

How does he survive without having to do the husbandly thing with his wife when he doesn't want to? Take a look...

What's the matter, dear, don't you feel good?

I'm fine! I was just trying to snuggle up to you...

But you did it in such an **awkward** way, I thought you weren't feeling good!

You think I'm **awkward?**

Not awkward...more like **clumsy!**

Our hero gets a good night's sleep and besides, why should he waste his romantic technique on his own wife when he's got such a great secretary! **Who?** Didn't you read the previous page? **That's** who!

Now, **why** does our young heroine keep such a **dirty room?** See for yourself...

This room is driving me **crazy!**

Oh, mom....

When I look at it, I think I'm having a nervous breakdown!

Golly, mom...

Her mother's refusal to go into her room is the **nicest** thing the old lady can do for her daughter! That's because the daughter's **boyfriend** has been living in her room for the past six months and no one in the house knows about it! How's she surviving? Not bad, huh!!

SURVIVAL QUIZ II

Well, you did pretty lousy on the **first** Survival Quiz! Want a second chance, huh? Let's see how many of you out there really want another shot at it! A show of hands, please. **That** many, huh? Okay, but **this** time, use your dopey little heads, will you? It's embarrassing for me to discover my readers are so stupid...

When you get to school late and discover that your zipper doesn't work, you should:

a) Be the first person to give his *live* body to Science; b) Crawl to your seat on your stomach, telling the teacher you're practising for the Marines; c) Tell the teacher you're wearing your brother's pants by mistake. Let her think that he's the pervert.

ANSWER: a) But be prepared for a turndown, especially with that body!

Your class is going away for a ski weekend and your parents start giving the best looking fellow the Third Degree, you should:

a) Try and convince the fellow that you were really adopted; b) Watch with interest as your entire life flashes before your eyes; c) Tell your parents, "We're not going to do anything more than Dad does with his secretary at lunch hour or Mom does with the tennis pro after a lesson."

If you're in a movie theater with your mother and you're too young to go to the bathroom alone, what should you do when your mother wants to take you into the ladies' room?

a) Have a king sized fit; b) Tell her you'd love to go to the ladies' room and see what's going on; c) What's the difference, you're probably too young to be able to read this anyway.

If you come home later than you promised you would, you should:

a) Tell your folks you walked home rather than submit to the boy's overtures; b) Tell them you just dropped in to get your nightgown and you'll be going back to the motel; c) Both of the above.

ANSWER: c) If you want to see what real confusion looks like!

You play cards for money and you lose. How are you going to explain that to your folks? You could:

a) Tell them you were robbed by a near-sighted burglar who didn't notice your watch or your bike; b) You spent it on a present for both of them, but lost the present on the bus; c) Confess, they'll understand.

ANSWER: Hold everything. Forget the answer. I just want to say whoever thought up the last possible answer (c) is some kind of a ravin' maniac. Honesty to your folks? You must be joking! Go on to the next question! I'm too upset to discuss this one further!

It's Mothers' Day and you have forgotten to get the old girl a present. You could:

a) Run into traffic; b) Remind her that it's the thought, not the gift that counts (like she always says); c) Plan to eat cold cereal for dinner for a month.

HAPPY DAY MOM

ANSWER: Just for kicks, try (b); You'll get an idea of how much air there is between what she says and what she does.

If a friend should ever ask you to hold his seat in a movie theater while he gets popcorn, you should:

a) Say, "Pardon me, do I know you?"; b) Say, "Tell you what, *I'll* go and you hold my seat." c) Hold his seat and get into fist fights because friendship is a sacred trust.

ANSWER c), but I don't believe it for a minute!

You've taken an important message for your father from his boss, but you can't read what you wrote down. Maybe you should:

a) Drop the pad and run away from home; b) Go to a hypnotist and try to get the message from your subconscious; c) Tell him your sister took the message.

ANSWER c) Unless you don't have a sister. If you're an only child, tell them your handwriting is terrible because you have the "Only Child Syndrome." (They won't know what that is, either).

The dreamy guy holds your hand, but your nails are bitten down to the first knuckle. You should:

a) Tell him that you must have short nails to be a concert pianist; b) Say that being with him has made you so nervous you bit your nails for the first time in ten years; c) Tell him you had them pulled out by foreign agents when you refused to talk about your father's C.I.A. secrets.

ANSWER: Try c). If he believes that, he's not the guy for you. Or maybe he is!

You're playing ball against the wall of your room. Unknown to you, your father is having a sex fantasy nap in the other room. Your noise has awakened him. You should:

a) Run to the nearest church and claim sanctuary (for non-Catholics, check with friends for the meaning of this); b) Quickly lie on the floor and tell father you fainted and were pounding on the wall to get some help; c) Ask him how his sex fantasy went.

ANSWER: b). But it might be fun to see how he answers (c).

Your blind date shows up and he looks like something the cat dragged in, then out, then in. You might consider:

a) Throwing up on his shoes; b) Start picking your nose; c) Tell him that your sister had to leave without being able to call him. (Of course, you have no sister, but he doesn't know that).

A SURVIVAL PRIMER

Now, here's a section for either the young or the simple-minded! (The young **and** simpleminded should **really** love it!) It explains how some people survive in this world! Follow their examples and you'll always end up on your feet (which is wonderful, except late at night when you want to lie down! But who said the world is a perfect place—it just beats the alternative!)

See the fat, roly-poly man?
Why is he so fat and roly-poly?
Because in his line of work, he doesn't move a *muscle!*
Who is this immovable object?
He is a *Phys Ed teacher.*
Look how he makes kids run and jump and sweat
And smell!
He never runs or jumps or sweats or smells—
He just *sits.*
What kind of condition is he in?
Actually, he is in good condition—
For a *statue!*

Believe it or not, the Phys Ed teacher
is a college graduate!
What did he study in college?
Three years of *Pushups*, two years of
Situps and an intensive year of *Taking Showers!*
But the most important course he took was
"How To Feel Comfortable Being A Grown Man
And Working All Day In Your Underwear!"
Sometime Phys Ed teachers coach school teams.
Then students can see that not only doesn't he have any
Brawn, but he doesn't have any brains, either!
Phys Ed teachers aren't *born*—
They're *made!*—Very Badly! And should be recalled!

See the people running around
Like so many crazies?
They are known as *tenants!*
See the man who is calm as a
Cucumber (and is shaped the same way)?
He is the superintendent, or *super* for short.
But not for long!
Why is that?
Because right after Christmas, right after
Receiving Christmas presents,
He will *quit!*
The super is supposed to fix things in the building.
Those who believe that also believe in Santa Claus
And are usually put away in State homes!

See the super with his clip board.
He is supposed to make a note of things to be fixed.
Every night he fixes his clip board
By tearing out the notes he made during the day.
"Clean clip boards make clean consciences,"
he always says to his wife.
Who doesn't listen.
He doesn't care if she listens or not because
He's usually too drunk to give a damn!
No matter how bad the super is, he never gets fired.
He *always* survives!
That's because the owner of the building doesn't know
the first thing about running the building.
He is at the super's mercy.
Like the tenants.

See the adults?
See how upset they are?
Why are they upset?
It's part of their *job* to get upset!
They are *parents!*
They tell their children,
"You will drive me to an early grave!"
But, somehow, after all these years
They're not there yet!
Parents are great survivors.
When they make you feel that you have them
At death's door,
A call from a friend of theirs to go out to dinner will
Revive them *amazingly!*

Sanity is something that parents prize very highly.
They want to keep theirs, even while
Trying to rob you of *yours!*
How come after all the yelling and suffering they do,
They still have a grip on reality?
Parents may not be able to teach their children much,
But they can give lessons in *surviving!*
They have the great ability to survive
Your illnesses, your broken bones, your marks in school!
Isn't it odd that after all the terrible and rotten things
You've done to them all these years,
They're still around?

See the *smart* man at the TV network meeting?
Is he the man at the head of the table?
Is he the TV network president?
Nope!
The network president isn't very smart at all!
Otherwise he never would have to become
Network president!
And lose his job next season when the shows flop!
The smart man is the little brown-nose
Who only knows one word, "Yes!"
He will stay in his job, no matter *who* is
Network president!
He really knows how to survive the corporate battle!

What kind of a man is the survivor at the TV network?
He is someone who *never* has an opinion of his own!
He is someone who *never* tells you how he
Feels about this show or that!
If he did, he would be vulnerable
When the show he liked *plotzed!*
So he goes along for an entire career
Nodding his head when asked for support
By the current president until
The signs are clear
That the current president is on his way *out!*
Then his head stops *nodding*
As the president's head starts *rolling!*
How can a man live like this—with no conviction at all?
For over $75,000 a year, that's how!

See the confident official?
He is telling the media there is nothing to worry about!
There's just a small radiation leak in the power plant!
Does it pose a threat to health?
"Nonsense," says the official!
"People who live in the area will not be affected!"
So why are people so shook up?
Because the official is *lying!*
If you want to be a survivor in this life,
There is no better position than being an official!
The official who passed on the safety standards for this
defective power plant is still on the government payroll!
The official who lies to the press is still
On the government payroll!
What would happen to you if you were caught lying?
Nothing, if you were an official!

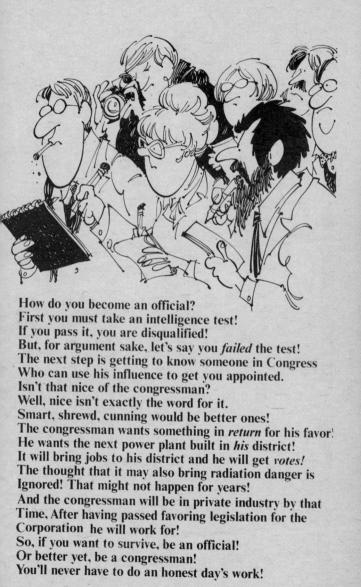

How do you become an official?
First you must take an intelligence test!
If you pass it, you are disqualified!
But, for argument sake, let's say you *failed* the test!
The next step is getting to know someone in Congress
Who can use his influence to get you appointed.
Isn't that nice of the congressman?
Well, nice isn't exactly the word for it.
Smart, shrewd, cunning would be better ones!
The congressman wants something in *return* for his favor!
He wants the next power plant built in *his* district!
It will bring jobs to his district and he will get *votes!*
The thought that it may also bring radiation danger is
Ignored! That might not happen for years!
And the congressman will be in private industry by that
Time, After having passed favoring legislation for the
Corporation he will work for!
So, if you want to survive, be an official!
Or better yet, be a congressman!
You'll never have to do an honest day's work!

ENEMIES III

So you thought we ran out of enemies, huh? Dummy!!

Next time you go into a deep **depression,** you should realize that your survival is being attacked! Like if you're at the beach and a fellow the same age as you looks like a young god while you look more like an old cherub, you might go into a depression! Hell, you certainly **should!** At times like these, it's best not to dwell on your inadequacies— it's also best not to go to the beach!

Don't blow your cork! Just punch out her kid
and let **her** get angry and lose **her** battle for survival.

The **doctor's office** can pose a serious
challenge to your survival! First you
wait forever to get an appointment,
and, when the lucky day arrives, you
wait forever in his outer office before he
condescends to see you! The strain of your
practicing patience while he practices
bad medicine can lead to crackups,
shattering your mental, emotional survival! One tip:
avoid getting sick, or, if you can't, get
sick on **weekends** when there are no doctors!

Sexual inadequacy is perhaps the gravest threat to your survival! I know it is to **mine!** You can't believe my wife… but enough about me, let's talk about **you!** The sexually aggressive female destroys the male confidence and if you only knew what it does to the male "Machismo," you'd plotz! Stay away from the sexually aggressive female unless you can handle her! If you can't, why not pass along her name and phone number to me c/o The Publisher!

Bite me, beat me, bruise me…

Would you settle for heavy hugging?

163

BATTLEGROUNDS III

BATTLEGROUND:
The Amusement Park

ANALYSIS: If you want to go on the roller coaster to impress your boy friend that you're a real good sport—*don't!* You will lose more points by *vomiting* than you will by *chickening out!* Also, consider your dry cleaning bills! Sometimes survival depends on *running away* from challenges!

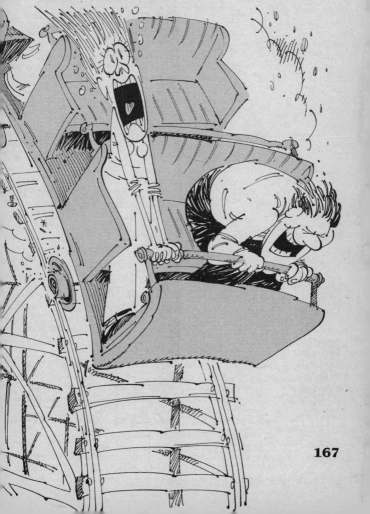

BATTLEGROUND:
The Telephone

ANALYSIS: The telephone, and the lack of privacy you have when you use it, is a true test of survival! If you can live with your nosey parents evesdropping on your important calls; questioning to whom you are talking; and griping that you're on too long when "that special fellow" calls—then you can withstand any assault on your survival mechanisms! Next step for you, *Sainthood!*

BATTLEGROUND:
Summer Camp

ANALYSIS: Your folks sent you away to *summer camp!* Wasn't that *unselfish* of them? *Bull!!* The reason they sent you was so that other children could be crueller to you than your folks are permitted to be, under *Child Abuse Laws!* Summer camp is a torment that tests both your *psychological* survival and your *physical* survival! Since it hardly pays to have one without the other, *preparation* is needed before you go to camp! Such exercises as running full speed, head down into a wall, or spending a whole afternoon with your sister, will help get you into shape for the agonies of summer camp!

BATTLEGROUND:
A Rock Concert

ANALYSIS: Survival, especially if you're still living with your parents, means staying out of *jail* at all costs! This might also mean staying out of *rock concerts* because the cops aren't *particular* who they bust! To them, *every* teenager looks like a *pothead!* So watch it when you go to see your favorite group or you could wind up trying to explain the whole mess through cell bars!

BATTLEGROUND:
The Department Store

ANALYSIS: Boredom Can Kill! Don't listen to what you've heard before, I'm telling you "Boredom Can Kill!" If you don't believe that, go with your mother to a *department store* sometime and wait for her to finish trying on dresses! You'll cut the waiting time considerably if you insist on going into the dressing room *with* her! You may also succeed in stopping *forever* her desire to take you!

There are those people among us who go on surviving, no matter **how little** they deserve it! To these unsung heroes, we now sing in the...

SURVIVOR'S HALL OF FAME

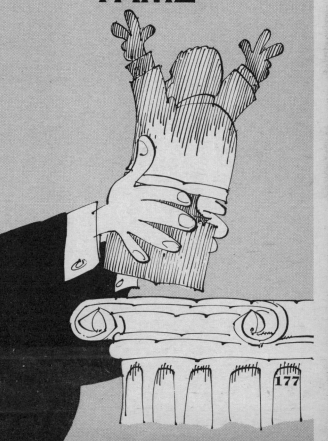

To the industrialists who pollute the air we breathe, but live far from their own factories in clean air, we award our Survivor's Hall of Fame Statuette...

To the criminal who will get out of jail in a year or two, while his victim will never get out of his wheel chair, we accord the Survivor Hall of Fame statuette...

One of the Survival All-Stars is the Lawyer.
No matter if his client wins or loses, he gets
paid...

For an example of survivorship at its best, we salute the American Doctor! He can, with pride, point to his successes! His failures, he buries...

To the unidentified idiot who gets away with playing his radio so loudly that others have their time ruined, The Survival Academy awards this Hall of Fame Statue...

To the drinker who thinks he can drive home after a party and who might get there, though others might not...

Among the great survivors of our time are the Military Brass! While they devise training schedules that could kill, they live a life of total creature comfort...

To the *big* drug pusher, not the little pusher who gets caught, The Survivor Hall of Fame awards this statuette, very begrudgingly...

To Chemistry Teachers the world over, who don't know what the hell they're doing, but keep doing it year after year, we award this statuette...

To the Big Three Auto Makers who keep making cars that must be recalled, but who manage to survive in business, we are all admiration...

To the master of survival, The Civil Service Worker, who keeps his job despite being lazy, indifferent and totally inefficient...

All hail the survival power of the Building Contractor, who stays on the job and stays and stays, while the home owner pays and pays and pays...

To the man who has the sheer guts to double park so you can't get out while he's visiting his girl and making out, we are all admiration...

To the Scoutmaster who manages to survive, even after his kids get lost, dunked, and covered with poison ivy, we award this token of our esteem...